HOCKEY TALK

This book is dedicated to Henri Richard.

Very special thanks to Al Mazlaveckas. Without his generous support *Hockey Talk* would not have been possible.

The author would also like to thank the following people for their assistance: Dakota McFadzean, David LeBlanc, Robert Lecker, Joanne Tilden, Henry Zurowski, Hugh Brodie, Oleg Dergachov, Lori Schubert, Margaret Goldik, Man-ki Hui, Michael Doerksen, Shawn Kuruneru, Alex McHattie, Ron Reusch, and Steve Lupovich.

—*John Goldner*

For my old man—my role model and the best artist I know; and to my little brother Patrick—who loved hockey enough for the two of us.

—*Ted Heeley*

HOCKEY TALK

The Language of Hockey from A–Z

JOHN GOLDNER

ILLUSTRATED BY TED HEELEY

WITH A FOREWORD BY MIKE LEONETTI

Fitzhenry & Whiteside

Published in Canada by Fitzhenry & Whiteside,
195 Allstate Parkway, Markham, Ontario L3R 4T8

Published in the United States by Fitzhenry & Whiteside,
311 Washington Street, Brighton, Massachusetts 02135

www.fitzhenry.ca   godwit@fitzhenry.ca

10 9 8 7 6 5 4 3 2 1

Library and Archives Canada Cataloguing in Publication

Goldner, John
Hockey talk: the language of hockey from A-Z / by John Goldner ;
illustrations by Ted Heeley; with a foreword by Mike Leonetti.

Includes short biographies of hockey commentators
who have helped to develop the language of hockey.

ISBN 978-1-55455-092-0

1. Hockey—Dictionaries, Juvenile. 2. Hockey—Terminology—Juvenile literature.
3. Sportscasters—Canada--Biography—Juvenile literature. I. Heeley, Ted, 1964–
II. Title.

GV847.25.G64 2009   j796.96203   C2009-904870-1

United States Cataloguing - in- Publicaion Data is avaiable from the Library of Congress

 Canada Council   Conseil des Arts
for the Arts   du Canada

Fitzhenry & Whiteside acknowledges with thanks the Canada Council for the Arts, the Government of Canada through the Book Publishing Industry Development Program (BPIDP), and the Ontario Arts Council for their support of our publishing program.

Cover and interior design by Fortunato Design Inc.
Hong Kong, China

Foreword

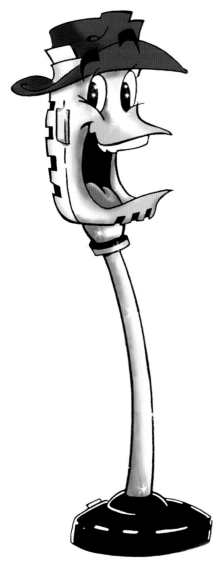

One of the great aspects of following sports is that each game has its own lingo. Words and phrases that are linked to a particular sport give that game colour, character, and a certain quality that cannot be found anywhere else. As a young boy who loved to watch and follow hockey, I can still recall the words of legendary broadcaster Foster Hewitt and his son Bill as they described the action for Toronto Maple Leaf games on radio and television. A player's three-goal game was termed a "hat trick," while a penalty call meant someone was "getting the gate." Montreal Canadiens play-by-play man, Danny Gallivan, (perhaps the best of all time) created terms like "spin-o-rama" and "cannonading" that are still used today. At the end of the game, we always waited for the "three-star selection."

Time has passed and the descriptions that go along with the fastest game in the world have changed. Certain players are now known as "grinders." Many goals are scored off a "one-timer" by shooters who have "wired it" into "the top shelf." Don Cherry of *Coach's Corner* does not like it when players now give each other a "face wash," but has come to accept that games are decided by "shootouts," and that some teams play a "neutral-zone trap." These phrases are all relatively new to the game of hockey, but they have added a great deal to a sport rich in tradition and history.

This book is not about learning how to play hockey or how to coach it, but anyone who reads it will learn more about the game and increase their enjoyment of the sport. You never know when a broadcaster will label something with a term or sentence that becomes used everywhere. But adding to the language of the game does not have to come from play-by-play people only. The next great hockey expression can come from anyone who enjoys the game of hockey—maybe even you!

—*Mike Leonetti*

The Language of Hockey

A

aerial A clearing technique. A defender lifts the puck high in the air and over the heads of attackers, so that it sails into the neutral zone and lands out of danger. This method of getting the puck out past the defensive blue line usually occurs when there is no safe pass to a teammate.

agitator A tough player who is likely to provoke a fight or at least irritate other players enough to cause them to take retaliatory penalties.

around-the-world glove save When a goaltender uses his glove hand to grab the puck out of the air with a wind-milling motion. Some might consider this to be a show-off move—but it looks impressive anyway.

in his attic In his head. If a player attempts to psyche out or distract a player on the other team, especially the goaltender, then he is trying to get *in his attic*. This ploy can involve taunting, boasting, reminding the opponent of a previous defeat or embarrassment, predicting a future defeat or embarrassment, etc.

B

back door An area near the net in the offensive zone, on the opposite side of where the puck is being played. *Villinov passes the puck to Lipman sneaking in the **back door**, and they catch the defense and the goaltender looking the wrong way.*

back end

"Dynamic Duo"

The back end tandem of Tim Horton and Alan Stanley helped the Toronto Maple Leafs to consecutive Stanley Cup victories in 1963, 1964, and 1965.

back end The defense. The **back end** can refer to the two defensemen on the ice or to the whole group of defensemen on a team. The **back end** can also be used to identify the defensive zone itself. *The Terriers' defense is playing very well in the **back end** tonight.*

backyard rink A homemade patch of ice, sometimes without any boards, usually right out behind the house. Lots of great hockey players began there. The most famous backyard rink is probably the one that Walter Gretzky built for his son, Wayne. A common thread concerning these labours of love is how difficult it was, or can be, to convince budding stars to come in for meals, to do homework, or to go to sleep at night.

bag skate A strenuous practice session. On occasion, a dissatisfied coach will force the whole team to do nothing but skate back and forth or around and around the rink, without pucks, for an extended time. A *bag skate* is usually a form of punishment after a poor game.

bagel A shutout. A goalie *gets a bagel* when he doesn't let in any goals. The team that doesn't score any goals *gets bageled*. The term is derived from the zero-like shape of the bagel.
See also: **donut** and **goose-egg**

ball hockey A hockey game played with a ball instead of a puck, and generally without skates. Ball hockey can be played almost anywhere: in a gym, on the road, on a driveway, in an empty parking lot, etc.
See also: **road hockey** and **shinny**

bang-bang play A quick combination play where the actions of two attackers happen quickly—for example, when there is a pass and shot before the defenders have a chance to react.
*Wallberg had no time to react in the Warthog net on that **bang-bang play** by the Terriers.*

barn An arena. Sometimes it's just a colourful term for any arena, no matter how modern and flashy it is—but if a rink is referred to as "a real barn" then it is usually pretty old and run-down with small, smelly dressing-rooms and possibly no heat.

benched Forced to sit out a shift or two. Sometimes the coach doesn't allow a player to take his regular turn on the ice because he is not happy with that player's effort or attitude. That player is then said to be **benched**.
See also: **riding the pine** and **warming the bench**

between the pipes In the net. The pipes refer to the heavy, red metal goal posts. *Goaltender Pierre LeGant played a solid game **between the pipes** tonight.*

biscuit The puck—which is flat, round, and shaped like a cookie. Not so tasty, though. But everybody likes a good biscuit; and everybody wants the puck.

blades Hockey skates. Putting on skates is *lacing on the **blades***. At the end of his career, a player who is retiring might say that he is *hanging up his **blades***.

blast A very hard shot *or* to take a very hard shot. *His **blast** went just wide of the net.*

(put the lines in the) blender Change the line combinations. Sometimes the coach decides to change his combinations of three forwards on the ice in order to mix things up and, hopefully, increase his team's offensive production in a game.

blew a tire Lost an edge. This refers to a player who fell to the ice, not as a result of any kind of interference or contact, but because his legs flew out from under him, perhaps because of some defect in his skate blade or simply from slipping. *McBrash was steaming down the wing until he just **blew a tire** and went sprawling.*

blueliners The two defensemen who are positioned at their own blue line to start the game or the period. They usually stay at or near the other blue line when their team controls the puck in the opponent's zone.

the bounces Lucky breaks. If you are *getting the **bounces*** then you are encountering good luck. The puck is made of hard rubber so there are a lot of bounces, one way or the other.

box (1) The penalty box. *Villinov gets two minutes in the **box** for slashing.*

(2) The box-shaped formation a team adopts in front of their own net when they are playing short-handed. The four defending players use this formation to try to keep the five opposing players outside of the key scoring zone in front of the goal.

box out Using the body defensively to block an opposing player from getting in a good scoring position in front of the net. *Villinov **boxes out** Bonhom, so the Terriers' captain can't get to the puck.*

Gene Hart was born in New York and grew up in South Jersey listening to Foster Hewitt broadcasting Toronto Maple Leaf hockey games on the radio. After serving time in the military, he began officiating high school football, baseball, and basketball games. He got into broadcasting by accident, after accepting an impromptu invitation to cover an amateur game in Trenton. When Philadelphia was granted an NHL expansion team in 1966, Hart submitted some audition tapes to the new team, which would be called the Flyers. Since the Flyers could not afford to hire a more experienced Canadian announcer, Hart got the job.

Hart became known as "the Voice" of the Philadelphia Flyers for the next 29 years until the end of the 1994–1995 season. He was noted for unabashedly defending the aggressive antics of those "Broad Street Bullies" teams from the 1970s, and was often a very vocal critic of league officiating. Over his career, Hart announced more than 2,000 NHL games, six separate Stanley Cups, five NHL All-Star games, and two NHL/Soviet Union All-Star series. For many years, Hart kept his job as a school teacher, travelling back from Flyers games in different cities just in time for the morning bell. His love of languages came in handy when European players joined the NHL with their unusual and often difficult-to-pronounce surnames.

Hart was best known for his signature phrase which he used at the end of games—"Good night and good hockey!" His call during the final moments of game six of the 1974 Stanley Cup Final is replayed often in Philadelphia: "Ladies and gentlemen, the Flyers are going to win the Stanley Cup! THE FLYER'S WIN THE STANLEY CUP! THE FLYERS WIN THE STANLEY CUP! THE FLYERS HAVE WON THE STANLEY CUP!"

In the early 1980s, Gene Hart was also one of the voices of the NHL on USA Network. He was inducted into the Hockey Hall of Fame in November 1997, receiving the Foster Hewitt Memorial Award. He came out of retirement in 1997 to announce for the Philadelphia Phantoms, the Flyers' minor league affiliate. He died in July of 1999.

brawl A fight that usually involves more than two players. ***Brawls*** were especially common throughout the 1970s in games involving the Philadelphia Flyers, a team that became known as the "Broad Street Bullies."

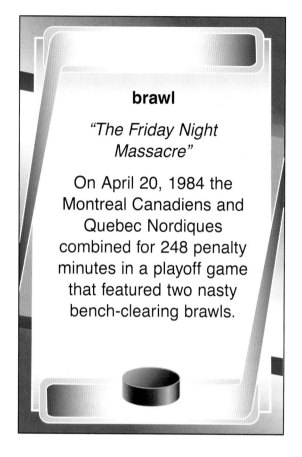

brawl

"The Friday Night Massacre"

On April 20, 1984 the Montreal Canadiens and Quebec Nordiques combined for 248 penalty minutes in a playoff game that featured two nasty bench-clearing brawls.

breakaway When a player with the puck is able to skate in unchallenged on the goaltender. This is an exciting play because the player on a ***breakaway*** gets a chance to use his puck-handling and shooting skills without any danger of being checked or impeded by a defender.

brick wall A particularly solid, unbeatable goaltender.

bulldozed the puck in Shoved the puck toward the net. When there is a scramble in front of the net, a player who has only a general idea of where the puck is may try to ***bulldoze*** the pile of players toward the goal line. However, goals are rarely scored this way because the referee usually blows his whistle first.

(the twine) bulges A puck shot hard to the back of the net appears almost to poke through the twine netting.

buries it Shoots the puck into the back of the net with authority, so that *the twine bulges*. *The goalie left the right side of the net wide open and Murray just **buried it**.*

butterfly style (goaltender)
A special goaltending technique. The goalie will drop to his knees and spread out his lower legs to block the bottom part of the net. His glove stays up in a catching position and his blocker hand covers the other side while holding his stick in front of his pads.

buzzer beater A last-second goal that is scored just before the end of a period. This often proves to be inspiring for a team that is trailing by two or three goals going into the next period.

buzzing Putting on the pressure around the opposing goal by keeping control of the puck, passing it around quickly, and perhaps getting a few close shots on net. This kind of team energy often leads to a goal. *The Terriers kept on **buzzing** the Warthogs' zone until Remedios finally put the puck in.*

cage The net. *Goaltender Pierre LeGant is **in the cage** for the Terriers tonight.*

camped out in front of the net Firmly set up by the opposition's net. A player who is ***camped out*** isn't going anywhere else anytime soon. This is a great position to be in for deflecting shots from the point or poking in rebounds.

cannon An extremely hard shot. *O'Flurry's **cannon** from the blue line blasted by the Warthogs' goalie.*

cannonading shot. This term was coined by the great broadcaster, Danny Gallivan (p. 88).
See also: **cannon**

can opener An illegal defensive technique that involves placing the stick between the legs of an opposing skater and rotating the shaft. This manoeuvre can be dangerous and often results in a two-minute tripping penalty. *Skillins goes down in a heap after McBrash gets a stick in there and gives him the **can opener**.*

carrying the piano Skating in slow, heavy strides. A player who is tired, often at the end of a hard shift, would be skating as though he is *carrying a piano* on his back. His coach might comment, *"I don't mind if you're carrying the piano; just don't stop to play it."*

carry the mail Move the puck. This term refers to the ability of a player to transport the puck swiftly up the ice using her skating skills alone. Also called "lugging the mail." *Look at Remedios go! She sure can carry the mail!*

catches iron Hits the goal post. Also *finds the iron* and *rings it off the red*.

centring pass A pass from the wing, the corner, or behind the net to the front of the net. *Skillins cuts around the defense on the far left side and passes to Remedios in front with a beautiful centring pass.*

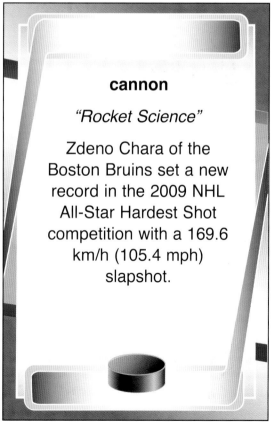

cannon

"Rocket Science"

Zdeno Chara of the Boston Bruins set a new record in the 2009 NHL All-Star Hardest Shot competition with a 169.6 km/h (105.4 mph) slapshot.

change up An off-speed shot. This term is borrowed from baseball and used in hockey to describe a shot which is much slower than the goaltender is expecting, often because the shooter has partially *fanned* on it. These tricky shots can be hard for a goalie to save. *See also:* **fanned**

changing on the fly Substituting players while the play is in progress. Players from the bench jump onto the ice to replace those coming off, without any stoppage in play. This is an aspect of the game that makes hockey unique because substitutions in almost all other sports take place when the action is stopped.

chase around the block Skate after another player in an unsuccessful attempt to catch up and take the puck away. *Remedios sped around the net and down the ice with the puck as Villinov* **chased her around the block**.

cheap shot A dirty hit with the stick or body on a player who is in a vulnerable position. This is the kind of action that often leads to retribution at some point. *McBrash's two-handed slash across Bonhom's wrist was a* **cheap shot**.

cheese cutters Old skates. They usually have dull blades and provide poor ankle support, both of which make them fairly useless for games. *"Why are you kids moving so slowly today?" asked Coach. "You look like you're wearing **cheese cutters**!"*

cherry-picker A player who is skating way ahead of the play, looking for a pass that could result in a quick breakaway goal. Sometimes, a coach will instruct a forward with a good shot to become a **cherry-picker** if the team needs a quick goal. But a player who does this habitually could be nothing more than a **floater**.

chess match A highly strategic game in which both coaches are trying to match up specific players on the ice. Sometimes they will try either to neutralize dangerous attackers or to align scorers against less effective checkers.

chiclets Teeth. Hard-hitting hockey players are famous for having several of these missing.

chippy Dirty play marked by any number of aggravating tactics, such as borderline late hits or sneaky stick work. It's a consistently aggressive attitude aimed at getting under the other team's skin. *The play is getting **chippy** out there, so we might see a fight pretty soon.*

chirping Complaining to the referees or bickering with a player on the other team. *Snarkman doesn't like the call, but he'd better stop **chirping** to the referee or he'll get an additional ten-minute misconduct.*

circle the wagons Skate around the net. When a player holds onto the puck and skates from one side of the rink all the way around the net and out the other side, then he has **circled the wagons**.

circus stop A spectacular save. This describes an acrobatic stop by the goaltender who has lunged for the puck from out of position, or otherwise demonstrated some exceptional feat of athleticism, in order to block a shot on goal.

climb the ladder Try to jump or reach up high to get the puck. When a player in the defensive end tries to clear the puck out of her end by lifting an *aerial* or by banking the puck off the glass, an opponent might **climb the ladder** to knock it down with his glove.

clear (1) Shoot the puck away from the defensive zone and out past the blue line. Sometimes it simply refers to moving the puck away from the front of the net. Also referred to as **clearing the zone** or **clearing the end**. *The puck was just lying there in the crease, but luckily LeGant was able to **clear** it in time. Then O'Flurry **cleared** it out of the Terriers' end.*

(2) Leave the offensive zone. Once the puck has been **cleared** from the zone, all the offensive players need to **clear** the zone as well before the puck can be carried back in. Otherwise the play will be called offside.

clinic Demonstration of superior skills. If a player is performing exceptionally well in a particular game, then a colour commentator might say, *"Skillins is putting on a **clinic** out there."*

clutch and grab Hold onto and slow down an opposing player. This sneaky style of play involves holding onto the opposition just long enough to slow them down without getting a penalty. It can result in a holding or interference penalty if the player does it too obviously and aggressively.

coast to coast End to end. A player who takes the puck from his own end and carries it all the way down the ice has gone *coast to coast*.

collapse Beat a strategic retreat. A team sometimes falls back to an area around their net when the opposition has the puck inside their zone. This way, with all those bodies in front, it's difficult for shooters to get pucks through. *The Terriers are **collapsing** in their end, so the Bulldogs can't find a clear shot at the net.*

connect the dots Complete the play. If the dots are the players, the method of connecting them is by accurate passes.

cough it up Give up the puck to the opposition. *Villinov passed the puck to Snarkman who **coughed it up** to Skillins on the blue line.*

crash the net Skate hard to the net. A team on the attack attempts to create traffic in front of the crease by driving aggressively to the net and sometimes bashing the goaltender.

credit card A free and easy game for one team. This term suggests that one team is having a fairly easy time at any point in the game because the other team isn't checking them hard enough. *O'Flurry has given the Warthogs' forwards a* **credit card** *tonight by not hitting them at all.*

cue Hockey stick. This infrequently used term is derived from **pool cue**, which is in turn sometimes called a stick.

cupcake A weak, ill-advised pass through the middle of the ice in the defensive zone which can be easily intercepted. It often results in a "sweet" scoring chance for the opposition.

cute Fancy. Sometimes the puck carrier attempts to make fancy, overly creative moves with the puck instead of making a simple play. The moves might look impressive at first, but they often result in the player losing control of the puck. *Coach always says, "Don't get* **cute** *with the puck when you're the last man back…shoot it out."*

cycling Skating the puck around. This is a method of moving the puck and holding onto it safely in the offensive zone. Players weave back and forth along the boards and behind the net, alternately leaving the puck for a teammate coming the other way. *The Warthogs are* **cycling** *very effectively in this game, and the Terriers are having a lot of trouble getting ahold of the puck.*

D

Fight. The combatants
ling to each other and
ound as they try to land
es.

e playoffs. *Now that
erriers have defeated the
hogs, they are going to
dance.*

o skate freely with the
κ. *Remedios **dances** in over
e blue line and passes the
uck up to Bonhom.*

ngle Stickhandle. The player in possession of the puck controls it very
deftly and cleverly in order to keep it away from the other team. A good
dangle combines feints and smooth skating to **deke** the defender.
*Skillins skates in over the blue line and **dangles** the puck past Villinov,
holding onto the puck before he passes it off to Bonhom in the slot.*

(in) **deep** Near or behind the red goal line. *The Warthogs shoot the puck
in deep. They want to keep it **deep** in the Terriers' end to keep them
from getting any chances to score this late in the game.*

deke A crafty stickhandling manoeuvre that moves the puck swiftly from
one side to another. A useful technique for carrying the puck around or
through obstacles and opponents. *Skillins rushes down the wing and
dekes McBrash by slipping the puck between his legs.*

Bob Cole was born in St. Johı Newfoundland, where he began ı broadcasting career at its local radı station, VOCM, in 1956. He eventu- ally became a hockey broadcaster for CBC Radio in 1969, and then joined *Hockey Night in Canada* in 1973.

Cole is, by his own admission, a Foster Hewitt disciple. In fact, he once sent a demo tape to his broadcast hero when he was first starting out. Hewitt met with Cole and tutored him in the use of changing voice levels to reflect different game situations.

Bob Cole is best known for using his own brand of catch phrases. He likes to use some old-fashioned expressions like *"Heavens to Betsy!"* and *"Oh Nelly!"* or the simple but effective *"Oh baby!"* and *"Scores!"* Other common Cole phrases include, *"He's a goalie, yes sir—and a good one at that!"*, *"Oh my, he was*

dish off Pass the puck. *Villinov cuts in over the blue line and **dishes off** to Snarkman for a hard shot on goal.*

dive An attempt by a player to trick the referee into penalizing the other team by flinging himself to the ice as a result of some slight interference or contact. If the referee is not fooled by the player's dramatic gesture, that player could end up getting a penalty for Unsportsmanlike Conduct. *McBrash takes a **dive** on the play as Bonhom steals the puck—and McBrash is going to get a penalty for that!*

donut Shutout.
See also: **bagel**

doorstep In front of the net. A player is right up close to the net when he is **on the doorstep** with the puck.

down low Behind the net and around into the corners. This is the area where key battles for possession of the puck often take place, especially after a ***dump-and-chase***.
See also: **(in) deep**

draw Face off. The referee drops the puck and two players (usually the centres) battle briefly for possession.

draw a penalty Cause an opposing player to take a penalty because he does something illegal to you. A player who is in a good position to score or make a play will sometimes ***draw a penalty*** when an opposing player has no choice but to hook, hold, trip, or interfere in order to stop him. *Bonhom uses his strength in front of the net to **draw the penalty** as McBrash has to haul him down to prevent a scoring opportunity.*

drop pass A short back-pass to a teammate supposedly skating right behind. This sometimes comes without looking, so it's a slightly risky play that can get you **benched** if the puck goes straight to an opposing backchecker instead.

dropping the gloves Preparing to fight. This is what players do just after they let go of their sticks (hopefully) and before they begin to **dance**. This term can also refer to the fight itself. *After that hit in the corner, O'Flurry looks like he's ready to **drop the gloves**.*

dump and chase Shoot the puck in and skate after it. This tactic is an effective way for the offensive team to get the puck in **deep** in the other team's zone. They will fire it in hard from outside the blue line, in the hope of regaining possession of the puck before the other team can get to it.

E

empty-net goal A goal scored on the opposition's empty net after their goalie has gone to the bench.
See also: **extra attacker** and **pulling the goalie**

enforcer A very tough player whose job it is to protect his (more skilful) teammates. This specialist is expected to fight anybody on the other team who attempts to intimidate anybody on his team. The enforcer's ability to score an occasional goal is a bonus—but not necessarily a prerequisite for the job.
See also: **goon** and **riding shotgun**

extra attacker A sixth player, usually a forward, who replaces the goalie on the ice. A team trailing by a goal, or even two, with little time left in the game will often remove their goaltender in favour of an extra skater. *Trailing 3-2, Wallberg races to the bench and the Warthogs send out an* **extra attacker** *in the hopes that she can help tie the game.*

F

face off The puck drop that begins a game or a period, or resumes play after a stoppage. Two players face each other at a red dot on the ice, the referee drops the puck, and the players battle for possession.

face wash An aggressive action in which one player rubs the palm of his glove into an opposing player's face. This contact occasionally transpires after a whistle when one player is displeased with an opponent or wants to provoke a fight.

fan on the shot When a player attempts to shoot the puck and misses it altogether. Of course, this can be embarrassing. *Klutski winds up in front of the open net but **fans on the shot**.*

far side The (small) part of the net a shooter can see on the opposite side from which he is shooting. *Lombardi speeds down the right wing and catches the **far side** with a quick wristshot.*

feed A short pass to a teammate who is in a good position to score, usually near the net. *Skillins **feeds** the puck to Remedios in front of the goal. Remedios picks up the **feed** from Skillins in front of the net and shoots it in.*

fire-wagon hockey Fast-skating, passionate hockey. The emphasis here is on offensive output resulting from a high-tempo attack which features a lot of skill and a certain degree of flair. The term was originally coined by Danny Gallivan to describe the style of the Montreal Canadiens in the 1950s, with legendary stars such as Maurice "Rocket" Richard, Jean Beliveau, Bernard "Boom Boom" Geoffreon, Dickie Moore and Henri "Pocket Rocket" Richard. This Habs tradition was carried on in the 60s and 70s by speedsters like Yvan Cournoyer and Guy Lafleur.

fishing Reaching for the puck. When a defender extends his stick in an ineffectual attempt to knock the puck off the attacker's stick, he is **fishing**.

five hole The gap between a goaltender's legs which provides a good target for a shot. The one, two, three, and four holes are not really holes at all—rather, they are the bottom and top corners of the net. *Villinov comes in on the breakaway and tries to go **five hole**, but LeGant gets the pads together in time to make the stop.*

flashing the leather Snagging the puck with the trapper or glove. The goaltender uses his big catching glove to quickly grab a hard shot which is headed for the net.

Don "Grapes" Cherry was born in Kingston, Ontario. He is one of the most popular—and controversial—figures in Canadian hockey.

Don Cherry was a professional hockey player for twenty years, spending most of his years in the American Hockey League. However, it wasn't until after he retired as a player that he became a star. As a coach, Cherry is best known for his stint with the NHL's Boston Bruins from 1974-1979. There, he led the Bruins to four straight division titles and two Stanley Cup Final appearances. In 1976, he took home the Jack Adams award as the NHL's Coach of the Year.

In 1980, he appeared as a guest on CBC's *Hockey Night in Canada*. The CBC liked him so much that they invited him back. Cherry soon had his own segment, *Coach's Corner*, a program where he showed game highlights and talked about anything that involved hockey. *Coach's Corner,* co-hosted by the unflappable Ron MacLean, turned Cherry into a national celebrity. Since then, he has been notorious for his colourful attire, his passion for hard-hitting hockey, and for the occasional controversial remark—usually directed at European players or those who think fighting doesn't belong in hockey.

Some of his trademark expressions include "All you kids out there…" and "…and everything like that." While he loves to trumpet the toughness of players with "big hearts" like Doug Gilmour and Wendel Clark, Cherry reserves his greatest praise for the "greatest hockey player that ever lived: Bobby Orr. And I love him!"

In addition to his hockey awards, Cherry has received recognition and distinction for his unwavering support of the Canadian Forces and Canadians in uniform. Whatever opinion viewers might have of the highly controversial Don Cherry, it's unlikely that anyone could complain that he is not entertaining. In 2004, Cherry was voted to the Top Ten list on the CBC's *The Greatest Canadian* series.

flamingo Chicken; as in faint of heart. This is an uncomplimentary way to describe a player who makes a timid attempt to block a shot, with one lower leg bent back, instead of fearlessly sprawling on the ice in the way of the blast. *Don Cherry is fond of saying disdainfully, "He comes out to block the shot and look at this—he's doing* **the flamingo**! *That's a disgrace."*

floater (1) A lackadaisical skater who does not give an all-out effort. This is generally a forward who skates around in a leisurely fashion, ahead of the play, waiting for his teammates to pass the puck up to him.

(2) A weak shot that drifts harmlessly in the direction of the net. Players will sometimes yell "float" to tease a buddy who has let go an unimpressive slapshot on the practice rink.

fly-by A deceptive "passing-play" manoeuvre. One player, usually a defenseman, stops up with the puck behind his own net while everyone gets organized for a rush. Then a forward on the same team will skate by him as though she's about to pick up the puck—but she doesn't. The defense then takes or shoots the puck in the opposite direction. For a moment, the opposing team isn't sure which direction the play is going to go. *O'Flurry has the puck behind the net...Remedios comes around on the **fly-by**, and now O'Flurry sends it up the other wing to Bonhom.*

flying Skating fast. *The Terriers are **flying** tonight, especially Skillins. He can really **fly**!*

flying

"Speed Demon"

Mike Gartner set the record for fastest skater at the 1996 NHL All-Star Game, completing one lap around the rink in 13.386 seconds.

freezing the puck Preventing the puck from being played. The puck is most often frozen along the boards when it is wedged between any number of sticks and skates. The referee will eventually blow the whistle and have a face off at the nearest face-off circle. The goalie may also *freeze the puck* in his crease by smothering it under his pads or trapper.

freight-trained Bowled over in the open ice by an onrushing adversary. *McBrash crosses the blue line and cuts in with his head down. Then he just gets **freight-trained** by O'Flurry.*
See also: **lights of the train coming** and **trolley tracks**

G

garbage goal An inelegant goal that is scored as a result of crashing the net and shooting in a rebound, or banging the puck into the net during a scramble. It might not come from a pretty passing play or nifty **deke**, but it still counts!

gauntlets Hockey gloves. This term was used more often in the past. Whereas knights of old threw down the **gauntlet** as a challenge, hockey players today usually drop their gloves as a signal to fight.

getting on the puck Pressuring the opposing puck carrier and hustling after loose pucks. *The Flyers are winning possession tonight by really* **getting on the puck**.
See also: **hustle**

getting the gate Getting a penalty. There is a gate to the penalty box that opens to let the offending player in. Every now and then it's slammed shut if the penalized player doesn't agree with the referee's call. *Villinov will* **get the gate** *for tripping Bonhom coming out of the corner.*

ghost A high-scoring player who has suddenly become so unproductive that he has virtually disappeared. These apparitions are particularly vexing to a coach during the playoffs. *Morrison had a great regular season with forty-five goals, but he's been a* **ghost** *in the playoffs.*

give-and-go A nifty pass-and-skate exchange between two attacking players. The first skater slides the puck to a teammate. While the defender turns his attention to the new puck carrier, the man who has passed the puck darts for open space and looks for a quick return pass.

Foster Hewitt, the man who first delivered live hockey play-by-play into the homes of North American hockey fans, was born in Toronto, Ontario. He remained a fixture on radio and television hockey broadcasts for several decades.

Hewitt became interested in radio at a very early age. He worked for a radio manufacturer until he took a job as a reporter at the Toronto Star. He broadcast his first hockey game in 1923 at the request of his employers when he was only 20 years old. The small, ice-level booth had no air holes, and the rookie reporter almost suffocated by the end of each game. Despite his discomfort, listeners enjoyed the game-calling experience so much that they wrote several letters of appreciation. Thus, Hewitt was asked to become a full-time announcer.

As the voice of *Hockey Night in Canada* and the Toronto Maple Leafs, Foster became the most famous play-by-play announcer in the game. He began each game with his signature sign-on, "Hello, Canada, and hockey fans in the United States and Newfoundland," and he was the first to use the phrase, "He shoots, he scores!" In 1972 he announced the epic Summit Series between Canada and Russia, and his description of Paul Henderson's winning goal has been immortalized in Canadian history. Hewitt called hockey games on radio and television until 1963, forty years after he began hockey broadcasting. Afterwards, he handed over the television duties to his son, but he remained as the radio announcer on his own station in Toronto, voicing Maple Leafs games until his retirement in 1978.

Foster died in 1982, but he received several honours in his lifetime, including the Order of Canada and induction into the Hockey Hall of Fame. The Foster Hewitt Memorial Award is given to broadcasters by the Hall of Fame, and the media gondola in Toronto's Air Canada Centre arena is also named after him.

give the what-for Retaliate. *Lipman slashed at O'Flurry's shins, and O'Flurry gave him the what-for in return.*

giveaway A turnover causing the puck to be surrendered to the other team without a battle, usually as a result of a bad pass.

glass Short for Plexiglas. There is Plexiglas around the corners and ends of the rink to keep the puck in play and protect the crowd. A good play in the defensive zone is to get the puck out past the blue line by shooting it up and along the *glass*.

go Fight. If one player says to another, "Do you want to *go*?" it's an invitation to *dance*. At that point there is usually a fight. After the fight it can be said that they *went*.

golden opportunity An excellent chance to score. *Oh! Klutzki just had a golden opportunity all alone in front of the net, but he shot it wide.*

gondola The broadcaster's booth high up in the rafters of an arena.

Up in the air

Broadcaster Foster Hewitt was invited to design the first broadcast booth at Maple Leaf Gardens. He decided that a bird's-eye view would provide the best vantage point for play-by-play commentary. A reporter remarked to him that the new booth looked like a gondola—the cabin suspended from the bottom of a blimp—and the name stuck.

NA NA NA NA! HEY HEY HEY—GOODBYE!

good-bye song A mainly wordless chant. Home fans often start singing the *good-bye song* late in a game if the visitors are clearly losing. It's especially popular in the playoffs when the visiting team is about to be eliminated.

good hands Excellent shooting skills. A player with *good hands* is able to shoot the puck very quickly when the opportunity arises. *The puck comes out to Skillins in front and he shows those **good hands** by putting a hard shot on the net right away.*

good stick The ability to effectively poke check and knock the puck off an opponent's blade. *Morrison tries to cut in front of the net, but Bonhom with the **good stick** knocks the puck away.*

goon A tough guy with relatively little talent whose main function is to fight. He tends to take a lot of *cheap-shot* penalties as well. This type of player was more common during the days of *bench-clearing brawls*, which are no longer tolerated.

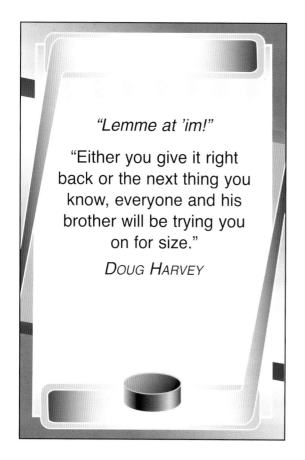

"Lemme at 'im!"

"Either you give it right back or the next thing you know, everyone and his brother will be trying you on for size."

Doug Harvey

goose egg A shutout. Also called a **bagel** or a **donut**. *There goes the siren; the Terriers win 2-0 and LeGant gets the **goose egg**.*

grinders Sturdy, gritty players who may not score very often, but who do a lot of hard work along the boards and in the corners. A forward unit employing all three players of this type is sometimes called a **grind** line. *The Warthogs have a lot of skilled players in their line-up, but it's the **grinders** who make the difference in the playoffs.*

H

hack (1) A reckless player who often wields his stick viciously.

(2) The act of chopping at an opposing player with the stick. *McBrash **hacks** Skillins on the arm—and he's going to get a slashing penalty for that.*

Not again!

half boards An area of the ice in the offensive zone approximately mid-way between the goal line and the blue line, near the boards. Often a player will take up this position with his team on the power play. *Skillins wins the face off and sends the puck up to O'Flurry on the **half boards**.*

handcuffed When a goalie can't get hold of a blast to the inside wrist part of his catching glove. *Here's a hard drive from the point—Wallberg is **handcuffed** on it and the puck drops in the net!*

hard around A hard shot that goes around the boards behind the net or in the corner. This shot is usually used in the defensive zone by a player who is attempting to clear the puck out over the blue line.

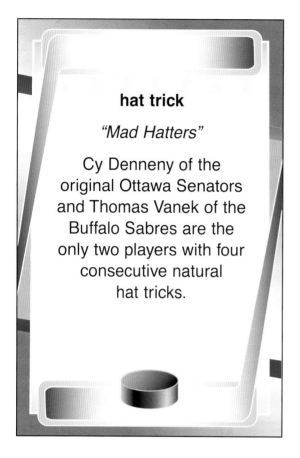

hat trick

"Mad Hatters"

Cy Denneny of the original Ottawa Senators and Thomas Vanek of the Buffalo Sabres are the only two players with four consecutive natural hat tricks.

hat trick Three goals by the same player in one game. As soon as that happens, the most enthusiastic fans traditionally throw their hats on the ice for the prolific marksman. A *natural **hat trick***, which is quite rare, occurs when a player scores his three goals all in a row, with no other player scoring a goal in between. The *Gordie Howe **hat trick***, however, is a different sort altogether. His specialty was to rack up a goal, an assist, and a fight all in one game.

head on a swivel Looking all around. A player will need to have his ***head on a swivel*** when he is going into the corner for the puck, with one or more opponents chasing after him—otherwise he could get checked or hurt.

headman the puck Pass the puck up the ice—specifically to a teammate who is rushing farther ahead. *Bonhom has it at the centre line —now he **headmans the puck** to Skillins as he rushes it into the Warthogs' zone.*
See also: **stretch pass**

heads-up play A particularly alert decision that a player makes with—or sometimes without—the puck. Keeping your head up and looking all around is very important in hockey, especially at higher competitive levels. It can affect your safety and your ability to **see the ice**.

heavy shot Hard shot. If a player is said to have a **heavy shot**, it means he can shoot the puck very hard. *O'Flurry is one of the best shooters from the point— he has such a **heavy shot**!*

helicopter job A flying stick that spins around in the air like a propeller. Usually, this flying stick belongs to the victim of a crushing, **open-ice hit**.

helper An assist.

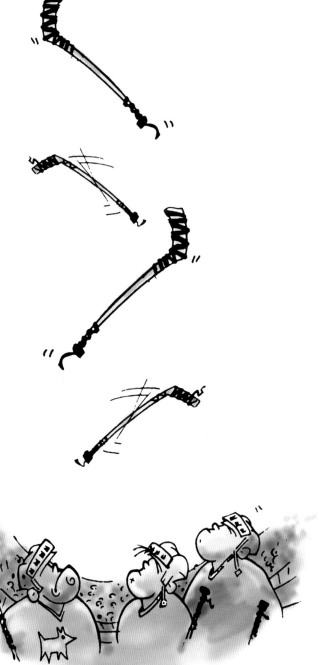

hitting the logo Shooting the puck at the goaltender—right in the middle of his chest. Of course, that is never where the shooter wants it to go. *Morrison has a great chance here, but unfortunately he **hits the logo** on LeGant.*

hogging the puck Selfishly holding onto the puck at length, rather than passing it to a team-mate who is in a better position. Somebody who does this a lot is called a ***puck hog***, or simply a ***hog***.

(getting the) **hook** When a goal-tender is pulled from the game and replaced with another goalie, usually because he or she is having a bad game. *Wallberg is **getting the hook** from his coach after giving up four goals on twelve shots late in the first period.*

hot shot (1) A very hard slapshot or wristshot on or at the net.

(2) A flashy, confident young player.

hung out to dry Left alone to fend for himself. When a team gets caught up the ice or otherwise abandons their goalie, it often results in a goal. *The defense has really hung Wallberg **out to dry**.*

hustle Work hard. This is a word that is hollered a lot in hockey, especially by coaches at players, as an exhortation to keep moving. *C'mon kids!* ***Hustle, hustle, hustle!!***

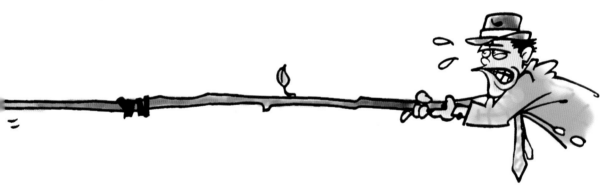

Fred Cusick was a former United States Navy lieutenant who went on to become the radio and television play-by-play broadcaster for the Boston Bruins, starting in 1952. Cusick was the voice of the very first network telecast of an NHL game in January 1957. He worked the NHL Game of the Week on CBS for four years and called every one of Bobby Orr's career games in Boston. As a young child, he watched his first hockey game at the Boston Garden in 1929: years later, in 1995, he called the last game that the Bruins would play at the Garden before the building was closed down. On that last day at the Garden, he said, "I've seen [Eddie] Shore and Orr—and you can't ask for much more…"

There was a subtle sense of urgency to the sound of Cusick's voice which was well suited to the game of hockey. It was particularly effective for covering the dynamic Bruins teams of the early to mid-seventies, with stars like Phil Esposito, Johnny

Bucyk, Derek Sanderson, and Bobby Orr. His signature phrase was a simple one—*"SCORE!"* He often summarized a great play with an enthusiastic *"What a goal by ..."* or *"What a save by…"*

Some of Cusick's truly memorable moments involved Bruin defenseman Bobby Orr, one of the most exciting players of all time.

In a game against the New York Rangers, the Boston goaltender stopped a shot by Brad Park and was out of position, leaving an open net for Park's rebound—but Bobby Orr dove across the crease to block the shot. Cusick couldn't believe it. "What a stop by Bobby Orr!" he exclaimed. "You've never seen anything like that!"

Cusick's favourite broadcasting moment, however, came on Mother's Day, May 10th, 1970, when he described one of the most famous plays in hockey history. "Bobby Orr…behind the net to Sanderson…to Orr, BOBBY ORR! SCORE! AND THE BOSTON BRUINS WIN THE STANLEY CUP! Bobby Orr, their 22-year-old sensation scores after 40 seconds of overtime!"

Fred Cusick won the Lester Patrick Trophy in 1988 for outstanding service to hockey in the United States. He was included among the first broadcasters to be inducted into the Hockey Hall of Fame, along with Danny Gallivan, Foster Hewitt and René Lecavalier.

I

ice breaker The first goal of the contest, especially when the game has been scoreless for a considerable length of time. *It was a scoreless first period between the Warthogs and the Terriers, but Remedios finally gets the **ice breaker** early in the second for the home team.*

ice is tilted The game is one-sided. In other words, one team is dominating the action so much that a lot of the play is taking place in their opponent's end of the rink. *The **ice seems to be tilted** in favour of the home team as the Terriers lead the Warthogs 2-0.*

ice time The amount of time, measured in minutes, which any given player spends on the ice during a game. The best players get the most **ice time**. *Villinov has played over twenty minutes tonight, so she certainly can't complain about her **ice time**.*

insurance goal Extra goal. When a team is leading by just one goal in the latter stages of a game, they would like to score one more, supposedly to ensure the victory.

J

(in) jail Lacking room to make an effective play. When a player has made the wrong decision with the puck so that he can no longer make a good pass, or he has no skating room, then he is *in jail*.

Johnny-on-the-spot In the right place at the right time. This refers to an opportunistic player who is, for example, there at the net to bang a loose puck into the open cage. *Wallberg blocks the shot, but Bonhom is **Johnny-on-the-spot** to bang in the rebound.*

juggling lines Changing forward combinations. Often a coach will switch his forwards around and put them with new linemates to generate offense when a team isn't scoring. *The Warthogs haven't scored a goal in the last five periods, so Coach Martin is **juggling his lines** now. See also:* (putting lines in the) **blender**

jump Energy and enthusiasm. This word is used to describe a team that comes out at the start of a game or period and seems to be skating very fast and play-ing with a lot of energy. *The Warthogs are down two goals, but they've come out with a lot of **jump** to start this third period.*

K

keep-away (1) Stick-handling the puck so skilfully that no-one else can get it.

(2) A little practice game where two or more players try to retain the puck by stick-handling around each other.

keep it alive Hold the puck in the offensive zone right at the blue line. Whenever a team has possession inside the opposition blue line, they want to do everything possible to prevent the defenders from getting the puck out, in which case the attackers would have to **clear the zone**. *Lipman fires the puck off the boards, but O'Flurry knocks it down at the point and **keeps it alive**.*

kill a penalty Prevent the other team from scoring when your team has a player in the penalty box. The usual way of **killing a penalty** is to gain possession of the puck and immediately send it down the ice. The out-numbered players on the ice during this time are the *penalty killers*.

kitchen The goal crease. An opposing player who ventures into a goaltender's space is in his **kitchen**. Goaltenders do not appreciate the intrusion.

kitty-bar-the-door Playing a very conservative and cautious game once your team has the lead. In this situation, your team will focus on preventing the opposition from scoring by concentrating on the checking game. *The Terriers go into this third period with a two-goal lead. Let's see if they decide to play* **kitty-bar-the-door***.*

Mike Lange hails from Sacramento, California. He got his start as an announcer for both the San Diego Gulls and Phoenix Roadrunners of the Western Hockey League. He joined the Pittsburgh Penguins as a radio announcer in 1974. From 1975 until 2006, Lange served as the lead play-by-play man for the Penguins' hockey radio and television network, never missing a broadcast.

The "Voice of the Pittsburgh Penguins," Lange has long been considered one of the most entertaining broadcasters in North American sport. His announcing is marked by the sheer variety and number of his colourful calls, known as "Langeisms." Fans of Mike Lange have devoted countless internet sites to lists and discussions of the broadcaster's unique terms, including the following:

- You can buy Sam a drink and get his dog one, too!
- Scratch my back with a hacksaw!

- He beat (the goaltender) like a rented mule.
- He smoked him like a bad cigar.
- (The goaltender) doesn't know whether to cry or wind his watch.
- Get in the fast lane, Grandma, the bingo game is ready to roll!

He similarly uses picturesque phrases to describe the action between goals. If a player steals the puck then "he picked his pocket like he was walking down 5th Avenue." When a defender is badly beaten, the opposing puck carrier has "left him on the parkway going to the airport."

When former Penguins captain, the incomparable Mario Lemieux was having another big night, then Lange often said, "Lemieux is putting on the Ritz." Nowadays, he's likely to say, "Slap me silly, Sidney!" when Sidney Crosby makes a great play.

Lange's enthusiasm for Penguins hockey has never been more raucous than during the playoffs. In the 1992 Stanley Cup Finals between the Pittsburgh Penguins and the Chicago Blackhawks he exclaimed, "The Penguins have won the Stanley Cup! Oh, Lord Stanley, Lord Stanley—get me the BRANDY!"

At the end of game six of the 2009 Stanley Cup Finals, Pittsburgh's overtime goal forced a final seventh game against the Red Wings. Lange declared, "We'll meet you in the school-yard, baby, for all the marbles on Friday night in Detroit."

In 2001 Mike Lange received the Foster Hewitt Memorial Award for outstanding work as an NHL broadcaster. In 2006, he moved out of the Penguins television booth and took over the radio microphone.

L

labelled Shot the puck to a specific part of the net. *That shot was **labelled** for the top corner, but LeGant managed to knock it away just in time.*

laser beam A very hard and accurate shot.

layered screening More than one opposing player in the goaltender's line of vision, at different distances from the net. This makes it more difficult for the netminder to see the puck coming all the way.
See also: **screen**

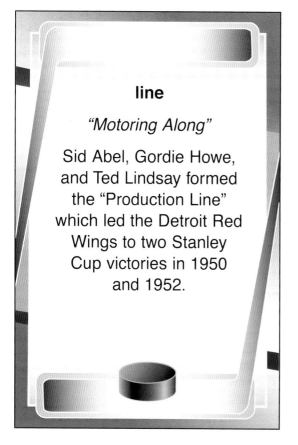

line

"Motoring Along"

Sid Abel, Gordie Howe, and Ted Lindsay formed the "Production Line" which led the Detroit Red Wings to two Stanley Cup victories in 1950 and 1952.

leather larceny Used to describe a great save by the goaltender with his glove. He has stolen a goal from the shooter.

lifter A shot raised off the ice. This is a popular technique that players used from the earliest days of the backyard and playground rinks.

light the lamp Score a goal. The lamp refers to the red goal light which the goal judge turns on whenever the puck crosses the goal line.

(see the) lights of the train coming An alert player who has his head up sees that he is about to receive a bodycheck. Thus, he can evade the hit or brace for the contact.

line (1) A trio of forwards made up of the centre, right wing, and left wing. They are linemates.

(2) An abbreviated reference to the blue line.

live grenade A weak pass that can easily be intercepted by the other team—with disastrous results.
See also: **cupcake**
Somehow a sweet baked good and a deadly explosive describe the same thing.

live puck A loose puck that is still in play since the referee hasn't blown the whistle yet. This term usually refers to the puck in the crease or along the boards when it is almost—but not quite—lost under a jumble of players, sticks, and equipment.

load up the cannon To lay the puck out and wind up for a big slapshot.
See also: **tees it up**

log jam (at the bench) A backed-up, crowded situation caused by players returning to the bench during the action while substitutes are jumping into the play at the same time. Occasionally, this confusion leads to a penalty for too many men on the ice, much to the chagrin of the coach.

loose change A puck lying around near the net which nobody has fired into the cage or cleared away.

lumber This refers to the raw material out of which hockey sticks have traditionally been made. Nowadays most players are using graphite or composite sticks. *Laying on the **lumber*** still describes a team that is playing a very rough game.

log jam

M

magic stick Describes the stick belonging to a player who is on a scoring streak.

malfunction at the junction When two players on the same team get tangled up. This clumsy play is usually the result of poor communication or confusion in the defensive zone. The "junction" is commonly a spot right around the net.

match-ups The coach decides which personnel he wants on the ice against certain opposition players. These are the *match-ups*. The advantage goes to the home team because they are allowed to decide last which players to put on the ice once the other team has sent out their players just before a face off.

moose A big, powerful forward who is difficult to bump off the puck or move away from the front of the net.

moves Slick stickhandling and shifty skating that are used to out-manoeuvre an opponent. *Skillins has some great moves, which makes him a tricky forward to stop.*

René Lecavalier (1918-1999) was born in Montreal, Quebec. He was best known as a Francophone broadcaster for Radio-Canada and the Montreal Canadiens.

Lecavalier was to the Canadiens what Foster Hewitt was to the Toronto Maple Leafs: the voice of the game. He began his broadcasting career in 1937 with Radio-Canada, the CBC's French-language station, presenting classical music concerts, variety shows, and cultural radio programs. He called the first hockey game televised by Radio-Canada in 1952, and went on to be the station's play-by-play announcer from 1952 to 1986. Lecavalier voiced the French-Canadian broadcasts of the National Hockey League games for over thirty years on *La soirée du hockey*, as the French version of *Hockey Night in Canada* is known. He also provided the play-by-play for the French telecast of the 1972 Summit Series between Canada and Russia.

While several Canadians are familiar with the English rendition of Paul Henderson's series-winning goal, French-Canadians would have been listening to Lecavalier's own interpretation: "*Et devant le but. Et le but de Henderson! Avec trente-quatre secondes encore!*"

During his time as a broadcaster, Lecavalier was more than just a hockey announcer. He also called several Olympic, Commonwealth, and Pan-American games, and he claimed that the opportunity to work on the 1976 Olympic Games in his hometown of Montreal was one of his proudest achievements. Still, he is credited for his influence in sports-casting—most importantly for creating a hockey language for francophones.

René Lecavalier received several honours in his lifetime including the Order of Canada. In 1984, he was also one of the first recipients of the Foster Hewitt Memorial Award presented by the Hockey Hall of Fame.

neutral zone The middle strip of the ice between the two blue lines. It is part of neither team's defensive zones. Sometimes it's referred to as the *neutral area* or *neutral territory*.

Neutral Zone

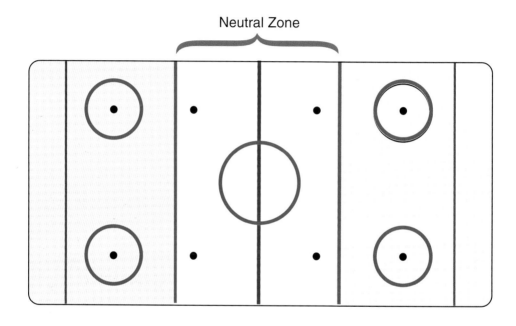

neutral-zone trap A much-ballyhooed defensive system which advocates crowding the ***neutral zone*** area between the blue lines with checkers in order to prevent the offense from scoring.

nobody home When there is no teammate in position for a set-up. *The winger passed it back to the point man—but there was **nobody home**.*

O

odd-man rush A rush up the ice with three attackers against two defenders, or two skaters against one.
See also: **rush**

off the hop Right after the start of the game, or in the first few minutes.
*The Terriers have taken the lead right **off the hop**.*

one-timer A fast shot by the shooter directly off a pass, without having stopped it first. This requires a lot of skill, but an effective **one-timer** can catch the goaltender out of position.

open ice Unobstructed space through the **neutral zone** and ahead of the attacker, into which he can freely move the puck. Or at any particular time, an area of the ice where there isn't much traffic.

open-ice hit A bodycheck which takes place in open space on the ice, rather than along the boards or in the corners.

open net A net that is completely, or almost completely, unguarded.
Open-net situations are usually created in two ways: the goalie can be temporarily out of position during the play; or the goalie may have been pulled in order to allow an **extra attacker** on the ice.

open wing A side of the ice where a left or right wing forward is open and ready to take a pass. *Remedios passes to the* **open wing** *and Skillins is there to pick up the puck.*

orchestrate the play When a creative puck handler controls the puck while expertly surveying the situation in order to set up the attack. *See also:* **quarterback**

outlet pass A pass, usually from the defense from behind her own blue line, to a teammate who is in a position to move the puck through the *neutral zone*.

P

paddle The part of the goalie stick which is wider from the heel of the blade up to the narrow part of the shaft. It does resemble a canoe paddle, somewhat. The wide paddle is especially useful for guarding across the bottom of the net in a "paddle-down" move by the goalie.

pad save A shot which is blocked by the goaltender using one of the long pads he wears on his legs.

(the) paint The blue ice or designated goal crease area in front of the net. An opposing player is never welcome *in the paint*—in fact, he may find himself being pushed out roughly by the goaltender or one of the defenders.

passengers Players who are not giving one hundred percent effort, so that their teammates seem to be "carrying" them.
See also: **floater** (1)

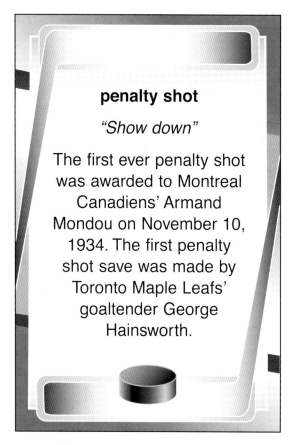

penalty shot

"Show down"

The first ever penalty shot was awarded to Montreal Canadiens' Armand Mondou on November 10, 1934. The first penalty shot save was made by Toronto Maple Leafs' goaltender George Hainsworth.

penalty kill The time during which a team has one or more players in the penalty box. The defenders must attempt to stop the other team from scoring while they are playing short-handed. Known as a "PK" for short.
See also: **killing a penalty**

penalty parade A game with a steady stream of players going in and out of the penalty box.

penalty shot An open-ice break-away opportunity awarded to a player who was tripped, hooked, or otherwise illegally interfered with, when that player already had a clear and open breakaway opportunity during the play. A penalty shot can also be awarded if one of the defending players (not the goalie) uses his glove to cover the puck in his own crease. During a penalty shot, only the goalie is allowed to defend the net. He or she cannot move from the goal line until the player has begun to skate with the puck from centre ice.

pest An aggravating player who effectively gets under the skin of the opposition, and who may eventually *draw a penalty* because of it.

pestered Closely checked.

perimeter player A soft, weak forward player who doesn't like to go to the net or position himself in front where it can get a bit rough.

picked his pocket When a player steals the puck cleanly from a surprised opponent, usually by skating up from behind and lifting the unsuspecting victim's stick. The player losing the puck has **had his pocket picked.**

penalty parade

picking cherries Easy glove saves for the goalie, because there is nobody to **screen** his view of the shot. (Not to be confused with *cherry-picking*—see **cherry-picker.**)

pick-up hockey An informal game which takes place in an arena or outdoors. Either way, the players have just shown up and are not part of an organized team or league. Sometimes, sides are chosen by throwing all the sticks in the centre and then tossing them one at a time in opposite directions.

pinballs around Ricochets or bounces unpredictably. The puck often **pinballs around** off the end boards when a player tries to shoot it hard in an attempt to **clear the zone.**

"HOWIE" MEEKER

Howard "Howie" Meeker was born in Kitchener, Ontario, and spent several years as a right-winger in the National Hockey League. He eventually worked as a coach, general manager, and television sports announcer.

Howie played hockey as a youth, but served with the Canadian Armed Forces during World War II before joining the Toronto Maple Leafs for the 1946-47 season. He won the Calder Memorial Trophy as an outstanding rookie that year, beating out players such as Gordie Howe. He won four Stanley Cups with the Maple Leafs and played in three All-Star games before retiring from the NHL. He went on to coach the Pittsburgh Hornets and the Maple Leafs and briefly served as the general manager in Toronto.

Beginning in the 1970s, Meeker became better known to hockey fans as an analyst on *Hockey Night in Canada*. Over a broadcasting career that spanned thirty years, Meeker worked as a commentator on the 1972 Summit Series between Canada and Russia, and he became the first hockey broadcaster to use a telestrator (a device that allows broadcasters to "draw" on the screen) on replays. In later years, he worked for TSN, CTV, and NBC. He was noted for his signature phrase "Golly gee willikers!" During broadcasts, Meeker also tended to yell out, "Stop it right there!" and "Back it up!" so that the video technicians could cue up plays for him to use on his telestrator during intermissions.

He ran children's hockey skills camps in the summer, and the CBC televised the experience in over 100 episodes of *Howie Meeker's Hockey School*. Meeker is still known for challenging North American hockey programs that focus primarily on strength, size, and grit at the expense of technique and skills. He is an outspoken supporter of intelligent skill-players, showing preference for systems that teach youths how to "see the game." He wants all young hockey players to experience "the enjoyment of being creative with other partners in 20 shifts of hockey, 'win or lose' at any level, any age." (Howie Meeker in *The Ottawa Citizen*)

In 1998, Howie was honoured with the Foster Hewitt Memorial Award, entering the Hockey Hall of Fame in the Broadcaster category.

pinching in When a defenseman moves in from the blue line and up along the boards to keep the puck in the offensive zone—and maybe get a chance to score. This tactic can backfire if the puck gets by the player *pinching in*—that can lead to an *odd-man rush* and a scoring opportunity for the opposing team.

playing catch Several passes back and forth between the same two players, usually on the power play, as they look to create an opening.

point (1) The area just inside the blue line near the boards. In the offensive zone, the defense are usually positioned at the **points**, where they will try to keep the puck from crossing the blue line into the **neutral zone**.

(2) A goal or an assist is counted as one **point** in individual player scoring statistics. Also, two **points** are awarded for a win and one is earned for a tie (or an overtime loss in the NHL) in the team standings.

pond hockey A seminal image of the game as it has long been played on frozen ponds, rivers, and lakes across the snowy winter land. Maybe snow banks take the place of boards and perhaps two piles of snow

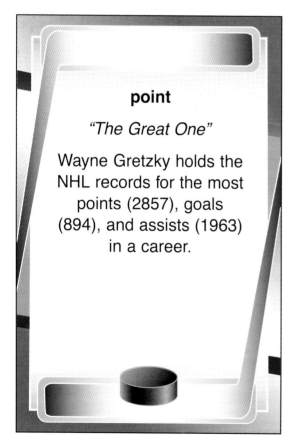

point

"The Great One"

Wayne Gretzky holds the NHL records for the most points (2857), goals (894), and assists (1963) in a career.

designate the nets. Nowadays pond hockey is also organized for teams of three skaters who play without padding and aim for nets which are less than a foot high.

post to post From one side of the net to the other. A good goaltender will need to move quickly from one post to the other in case of a quick cross-crease pass.

power forward A big centre or winger who uses his size to drive to the net or to establish position in front of it. This is also the kind of player who tends to win a lot of battles along the boards.

power play During a penalty, while one team has a player in the penalty box, the other team with the man-advantage goes on the *power play* or "PP" for short. This is the opposite of the *penalty kill*.

puck-drop The opening face-off at the start of a game.

puck has eyes Describes a shot which finds its way to the net through lots of traffic. Also called a "seeing-eye puck."

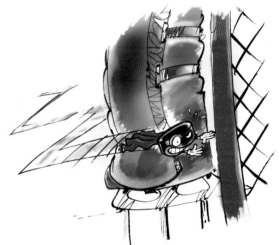

pulling the goaltender/goalie A strategy used by a coach in order to boost his or her team's chances to score a quick goal by replacing the goalie with an extra forward. This risky move usually occurs in the last minute or two of play when a team is losing by one or two goals.
See also: **extra attacker**

pulling the trigger Firing the puck. This term usually applies to a quick wristshot.

put that one in the memory bank Make a mental note. Whenever a player is beaten, or conversely beats his opponent, the play is filed away so that the next time they face each other in a similar situation there is some information to go on. *Morrison goes five hole on the breakaway—LeGant will have to **put that one in the memory bank**.*

Q

quarterback A term borrowed from football to characterize the key member of a top ***power-play*** unit who usually plays the ***point***. This player's job is to organize the rush from the back and ***orchestrate*** the attack in the offensive zone.

R

radio shot A shot that the goaltender only hears but does not see because he has been screened.

ragging the puck Holding onto the puck without the immediate intention of advancing it into scoring position. This is done by circling back to avoid checkers, for example, while killing a penalty.

rearguard Another term for the defense.

rebound A puck that has bounced back into the shooting area after hitting the goaltender, goalpost, glass, or boards. **Rebounds** create great scoring opportunities for players who are always ready in front of the net.

riding shotgun Acting as a protective enforcer. If there is an exceptionally valuable goal-scorer or playmaker on a team, the coach will not want that player to fight and risk an injury. A rugged linemate who is good at dropping the gloves will usually be on the ice at the same time in order to act as a bodyguard. *McBrash is **riding shotgun** with his captain, Villinov, in what promises to be a rough-and-tumble game.*

ring the boards Shoot the puck hard along the bottom of the boards, usually around the back of the net, from one corner to another. Sometimes called "rims."

rink rat A kid who spends a lot of time hanging around the arena because he loves to play hockey, or because he really likes watching it. Could be that he has a few friends on the team. Perhaps he just enjoys the french fries at the snack bar.

road hockey A game played on a relatively quiet street, wearing running shoes or boots, and using either an old tennis ball or a bright plastic ball instead of a puck. If a vehicle comes down the road, somebody shouts "Car!" and the light, portable nets are moved as everyone steps out of the way. Play resumes when the nets are replaced and someone else yells, "Game on!"

road map A battered face with many cuts and scrapes. *McBrash's face looks like a **road map** after that tough game.*

robbed Prevented from scoring an easy goal by a spectacular save. *Villinov had the open side of the net but was **robbed** by LeGant's acrobatic toe save!*
See also: **stoned** and **deny**

roof (1) The very top part of the net, from the front crossbar to the back.

(2) To score a goal by shooting the puck into the top part of the net. *Remedios* **roofed** *that shot over the goalie's shoulder.*

room (1) The space, or lack of space, available on the ice to skate and make plays. If one team is playing their positions well and covering the ice evenly, the announcer might say that *there's not a whole lot of* **room** *out there tonight* for the other team.

(2) The dressing room. Usually smelly, damp, and cramped, and littered with balls of leftover tape.

(3) The general atmosphere or attitude in the dressing room, especially referring to the sense of harmony (or lack of harmony) among the players. *You can just imagine* **the room** *after the Warthogs' latest loss.*

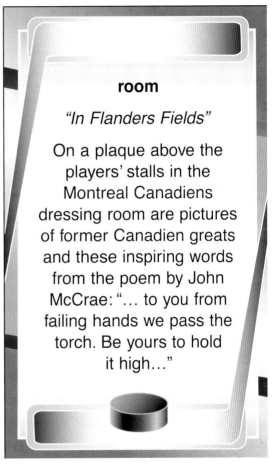

room

"In Flanders Fields"

On a plaque above the players' stalls in the Montreal Canadiens dressing room are pictures of former Canadien greats and these inspiring words from the poem by John McCrae: "… to you from failing hands we pass the torch. Be yours to hold it high…"

rubber The puck. The expression *He is seeing a lot of* **rubber** means that the goaltender is facing many shots.

run When a player charges across the ice and slams into an opponent with malice aforethought. An unsportsmanlike sort of hit.

Shoot here...   or here...   Too late!   Abandon hope...

run-and-gun A wide-open style of play with an emphasis on scoring lots of goals. This style is usually favoured by a team with many skilled offensive players—even if it allows the opposition a certain number of chances, too.

running around Chasing after the puck ineffectively in the defensive zone.
*The disorganized Warthogs are just **running around** after the puck and can't seem to get it away from the Terriers.*

run out of real estate An attacker has ***run out of real estate*** when his drive to the net has carried him too far in, so that he has actually crossed the goal line and has no angle left to shoot the puck in the cage.

rush An offensive attack that moves the puck up the ice quickly. This can be done by one player carrying it, two or more passing it, or any combination of the above. A team or player in that case is ***on the rush***.

Finis !

sales job When a player embellishes the effect of a foul, such as a high stick or an elbow to the head, in order to make sure the referee sees the infraction and calls a penalty.

sandpaper The gritty elements on any team, in the form of tenacious and tough players. These are the grinders, muckers, and pluggers who are so instrumental in winning.

saucer pass A nice pass which arrives flat on the ice, especially to a teammate who is in good position for a *one-timer*.

scramble A tangled mess of players in front of the net who are trying to get at a loose puck. Combatants fall down and sticks clash as everyone bangs away, while the goaltender flails around in the mayhem trying to smother the elusive disc.

scrambled face off A face off that results in neither centre being able to draw the puck cleanly back to a teammate. Instead, the puck remains sitting right near the point where it was dropped, as the wingers on both sides join in the fight for possession.

Rick "RJ" Jeanneret, the voice of the Buffalo Sabres, was born in St. Catharines, Ontario in 1942.

"RJ" (whose other nickname is "Rodney" because of his resemblance to the comedian Rodney Dangerfield) got his start calling the radio broadcast for the Junior A Niagara Falls Flyers hockey team in 1963. When the regular announcer fell ill, Jeanneret was there to fill in. After a year of working as a colour analyst, he began calling the play-by-play on a full-time basis.

Jeanneret has been the voice of the Sabres since the 1971-72 season, making him the longest-serving announcer in the NHL today. He calls the games for both television and radio audiences. His passion and vocal enthusiasm (and fondness for flashy suspenders) have made him a fan favourite both in Buffalo and across North America with several websites and links devoted to his classic calls. Some of his more memorable examples include the following:

"Call a cop! He robbed him blind!

"Top shelf! Where Momma hides the cookies!"

"The cookie monster strikes again!"

"'Tis the season! Fa-la-la-la-la-la-LaFontaine!"

Jeanneret has released two DVDs, *Roll the Highlight Film* and *Top Shelf*, both commemorating some of his most popular calls. The proceeds of these DVDs support various charitable causes.

Considering that he has called almost every game the Sabres have played since 1971, their second year as an NHL team, "RJ" is an integral part of the Buffalo team and its history. Rumours of Jeanneret's retirement have surfaced every year since the 2004-05 season, but he keeps putting it off for "one more year". "RJ" is still hoping to broadcast the Sabres' first Stanley Cup victory.

screen When a player or players from either team are positioned in front of the net, obstructing the goalie's view. An offensive player will try to do this deliberately—but unfortunately, a defensive player trying to help his goalie out can also end up blocking his vision of the puck.

scrum A gathering of the clans at close quarters after the whistle. At that point, players may participate in a certain amount of *chirping*, pushing, and *face washing*. Occasionally leads to a *dance*.

seam A gap or a space between defenders which is available to the attacking team. They can either carry the puck through or feed a pass to a teammate *in the seam*.

seeing the ice The ability to *see the ice* alludes to a player's hockey sense, in terms of knowing where teammates and opponents are at any given time and how the play is shaping up.

set up (1) Passing the puck off to a teammate who is then in a good position to score. *Remedios **sets up** Bonhom for a one-timer at the top of the circle.*

(2) The power play unit is **set up** in the offensive zone when it has possession of the puck and all the attackers are spread out effectively.

shadow Follow or cover an opponent. Occasionally, a coach will assign one of his best checkers to do nothing but follow the other team's top scorer all over the ice and attempt to take way his or her opportunity to get involved in the play.

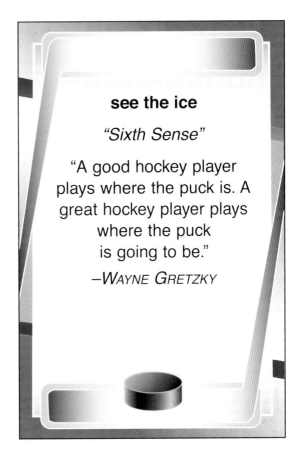

see the ice

"Sixth Sense"

"A good hockey player plays where the puck is. A great hockey player plays where the puck is going to be."

–WAYNE GRETZKY

shift One brief period of ice time during the game, usually a minute or so. A player who is double-shifted gets to play on two lines. *O'Flurry heads to the bench for a rest after working hard on the ice all through that **shift**.*

shinny An informal hockey game played on the ice with or without skates. Instead of a puck, players might choose to use an old tennis ball, a plastic hockey ball, or even a soft rubber puck.

shoot-in A shot into the offensive zone that comes from anywhere in the neutral zone. Most ***shoot-ins*** are fired around the boards, but sometimes they travel diagonally across the ice.
See also: **dump and chase**

shooting gallery The unfortunate goalie and his net area when they are being bombarded by a lot of shots.

shooting lane The unobstructed angles leading to the net, through which the opposing players can fire the puck.

shootout (1) A very high scoring game in which neither team seems overly concerned with defensive tactics. Coaches supposedly don't like shootouts, but the fans usually do. (2) A means of determining a winner if a game ends in a tie. Each team selects a certain number of shooters to take *breakaway* shots on the goalie. One by one, the shooters try to score. At the end of a predetermined number of shots, the team that has scored the most goals wins the game.

shortening the bench When a coach decides to use fewer of his available players during the game. He may go with only three forward lines exclusively, or just two pairs of defense. The idea is to give his best players more ice time.

shorthanded Playing with fewer players on the ice than the other team, usually as a result of a penalty.

shortie A goal scored while playing *shorthanded*.

short side Off at an angle, the
short side is that portion of the
net a shooter can see on the
same side from which he is
shooting.

shutdown defenseman
A top defensive player who is
deliberately matched up on the
ice against the best shooter
on the other team, in order to
prevent that player from having
an impact on the game.

stretch pass A long pass from
the defensive zone to a player
much farther up the ice.

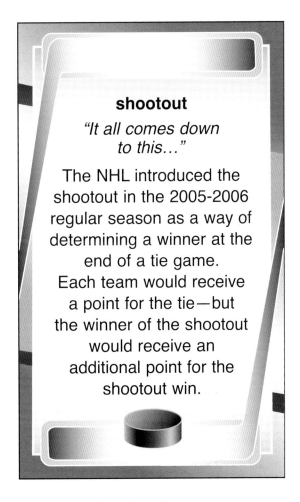

shootout

*"It all comes down
to this..."*

The NHL introduced the
shootout in the 2005-2006
regular season as a way of
determining a winner at the
end of a tie game.
Each team would receive
a point for the tie—but
the winner of the shootout
would receive an
additional point for the
shootout win.

shutting the door A goaltending
move that blocks off an opening and stops a shot from in close.
See also: **stoned**

sieve A playful but insulting term for a weak goaltender who generally
lets in a lot of goals, especially on weak shots.

silencer A crucial goal scored by the visiting team that silences a previously boisterous home crowd.

sin bin The penalty box. For a list of "Thou shalt nots" in hockey, consult a standard manual of rules.

six by four An open net for the shooter. The net measures six feet wide by four feet high.

slapper A slapshot.

slew foot The old *slew foot* is a sneaky way to trip an opposing player. The perpetrator slides his skate right up behind the back foot of the opponent and pulls forward, spilling him.

slot An unmarked area in front of the net, between the face-off circles. The *slot* is prime shooting territory, about fifteen to thirty feet out.

smashmouth hockey Hard-hitting, in-your-face hockey. It can still be a violent game, but professional hockey has begun to distance itself from this excessively rough kind of competition.

sniper A very accurate and hard shooter who is capable of scoring a lot of goals.

snow shower An upward spray of ice off the skates of a speedster who stops suddenly. A goalie who is down to freeze the puck occasionally gets the *snow shower*. Goalies don't like it—and the skater who showered him can get a penalty for unsportsmanlike conduct.

soccer play Using a skate to kick the puck to a teammate or to move it ahead. Resourceful players often do this along the boards if they can't get their stick on the disc. Occasionally called a "Pele."

soft hands The ability of a skilled player to make deft, light passes or shots.

softie A goal scored on a weak shot, or one from either a bad angle or far out. *The Warthogs have been sagging ever since Wallberg gave up a* **softie** *in the second period.*

solo mission An offensive attempt by one player alone on the rush, usually because her linemates have already gone to the bench on a change. *Kat Remedios is on a* **solo mission** *as she crosses the blue line and her linemates head to the bench.*

soft hands

"A Quick Tip for Soft Hands"

Off the ice, practice stick-handling with a golf ball. Keep your hands relaxed on the stick and tap the ball back and forth.

Danny Gallivan was born in Sydney, Nova Scotia, and went on to become the beloved English voice of the Montreal Canadiens from 1952 to 1984. His broadcast career began at a radio station in Antigonish where he worked while attending St. Francis Xavier University. After graduation he taught high school and spent some time in the Canadian Armed Forces.

Gallivan got his big break in 1950 when he was spotted by a CBC producer of *Hockey Night in Canada* during a junior hockey playoff game broadcast. *HNIC* asked him to fill in for a sick announcer. For over 30 years, Gallivan called more than 1,800 Canadiens games on both television and radio.

It was his command of the English language and the colourful adjectives he used that gave Gallivan such a distinctive style. He certainly invented some of the most memorable descriptions in the history of hockey broadcasting. "Cannonading drives" (hard shots) and "scintillating" or "hair-raising" saves became part of the hockey vocabulary. When the goalie snatched the puck out of the air with his glove, he often did so "in rapier-like fashion." Pucks were "gobbled up," passes were "feathered," and players "dipsy-doodled" over the blue line.

The term that is probably Gallivan's best-known concoction is the "spin-o-rama." Back in the 50s and 60s, it became trendy to add the suffix "rama" to the ends of words—for example, "Bowl-o-rama" or even "Laund-o-rama." As Gallivan told CBC Sports reporter Fred Walker, he was riding the team bus to Oakland and pondering how he could work "rama" into his hockey play-by-play. Later, when Serge Savard of the Canadiens did a 360-degree spin to avoid an opposing player, "spin-o-rama" sprang to mind. The "Savardian Spin-o-rama" was born. In fact, the word "spin-o-rama" is now an official entry in the *Canadian Oxford Dictionary*.

Danny Gallivan is a Foster Hewitt Memorial Award honoree in the Hockey Hall of Fame and a member of Canada's Sports Hall of Fame. He died in 1993.

spark plug A particularly determined or feisty player who is not necessarily the best on the squad, but who often ignites his teammates or comes up with a big goal.

sparkler Scintillating save by the goalie.

special teams The group of players who typically are assigned to play during *power plays* and *penalty-kills*.

spin-o-rama A fancy move by the puck carrier to change directions by spinning around, often on the backhand, in order to elude a check or take a shot.

splits An acrobatic move (like the one in gymnastics) where the goalie stretches his legs out from side to side to block a hard, low shot with the tip of his skate or the bottom of his pad.

squeezing the stick An indication that a player is feeling extra tense. Perhaps it's the pressure from a very important game or a playoff series. Or perhaps the player is battling through a difficult slump. *Lipman, with only one goal in the last fifteen games, has been* ***squeezing the stick*** *ever since the playoffs began.*

stacking the pads A goalkeeping technique for stopping a shot while the goalie is down on the ice. In a horizontal position on his side, he lifts his top leg and lays it on the side of his bottom one, so his pads are stacked to block more of the net. Sometimes called the ***two-pad stack.***

staged fight A scrap prearranged by a private agreement, usually between two enforcers, to ***drop the gloves*** and ***go*** right after the ensuing face off. This form of premeditated combat is under close scrutiny by the NHL.

standing on his head A great game performance by a goaltender who is making acrobatic saves and robbing shooters on chances that would normally go in. *LeGant really **stood on his head** in that game and earned a shutout.*

stand up A defensive tactic where a team lines up a number of players just outside their own blue line to prevent the opposition from gaining the zone easily.

stand-up goaltender A goaltender who prefers to remain in the upright position, if he can. Opposite to the **butterfly style**.

stapled to the boards or the glass Hit really hard into the boards. *See also:* **wallpapered**

stay-at-home defenseman A defender who does not often carry the puck very deep into the opposition zone. He chooses to remain back in his position and protect the goalie in his own end.

stoned Stopped from scoring in close to the net. The goaltender just doesn't give the shooter any room to put the puck in the net, and then blocks the shot from close range.

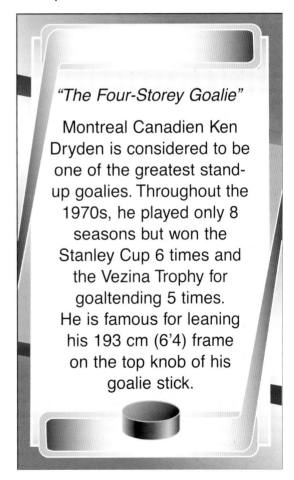

"The Four-Storey Goalie"

Montreal Canadien Ken Dryden is considered to be one of the greatest stand-up goalies. Throughout the 1970s, he played only 8 seasons but won the Stanley Cup 6 times and the Vezina Trophy for goaltending 5 times. He is famous for leaning his 193 cm (6'4) frame on the top knob of his goalie stick.

stripped If a player in the open ice has the puck taken from him, then he has been ***stripped of the puck***. *See also:* **picked his pocket**

submarine To hit an oncoming or unsuspecting opponent by crouching down low enough to upend him and flip him upside down.

sudden death When the score is tied after three periods of regulation time, the game moves into one or more periods of overtime. As soon as a goal is scored, regardless of how much time is left in the overtime period, the game is over. The play stops dead—the team that scored wins. The team that let the goal in loses. End of story. Lights out.

swimming A goaltender's inelegant attempt to propel himself to a better position by sliding his arms and legs around while he is caught lying flat on the ice.

T

tailgating Skating closely behind an opposing player all the way down the ice, perhaps even making some contact along the way.

take the foot off the gas Slow down and let up. Sometimes a team with a big lead will ease up, perhaps expecting that the other team will give up since the game is so far out of reach. Very dangerous— comebacks *do* happen!

take his number Make a note of who hit you. Following a big hit, the victim will look around to see who it was that levelled him. The idea is to extract some form of revenge later on in the game.

(on the) tape Most players tape the blades of their sticks. A good pass from one player's stick to another is *on the tape*. This is sometimes called a "tape-to-tape pass."

tap in An easy goal scored when the puck is sitting loose right near the goal line.

tee it up When a shooter has time to set the puck up nicely in front of him for a big slapshot.

ten-bell save A particularly great save.

three stars A long-standing tradition in which a member of the press or an announcer chooses the best three players of the game. Those players skate out on the ice one at a time and raise their sticks to the applause.

tic-tac-toe A very crisp and quick passing play between three players that results in a goal-scoring opportunity. If the puck goes in, it can be described as a *tic-tac-goal!*

tied up Closely checked, so that the player can't move the puck easily or take a good shot.

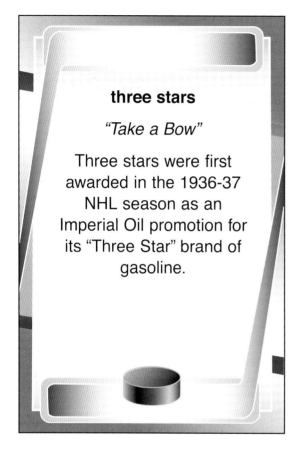

three stars

"Take a Bow"

Three stars were first awarded in the 1936-37 NHL season as an Imperial Oil promotion for its "Three Star" brand of gasoline.

tip in A goal scored by the deflection of a flying puck into the net by a player on the shooting team who is usually positioned in front of the net.

toe-drag move A tricky stickhandling manoeuvre. The blade of the stick is rotated up so that the shorter side is in flat contact with the ice, while the puck comes up flush behind it. Then the puck is quickly pulled back. This is fancy *dangling*.

toe save A save made with the toe part of the goalie's skate, deflecting the puck away.

top-shelf The upper part of the net. *Lipman tried to go **top-shelf** on LeGant but the goalie's quick glove caught the puck just in time.*

tomahawk chop A vicious, two-handed slash.

traffic A congestion of players in the same area of the ice, particularly one or more attackers going to the net or screening the goaltender.

trapped Held up or caught inside the opposition zone when the puck enters by crossing the blue line. This creates an offside situation.

trailer A player who joins the *rush* late, coming up from behind into open ice.

train wreck A heavy collision between two players coming hard from opposite directions. Also describes a team which is playing very poorly.

trapping Playing the *neutral-zone trap* style of defense.

trolley tracks An imaginary route inside the blue line, created when a player with the puck cuts sharply from either wing toward the centre, unfortunately with his head down. The trolley arrives in the form of a big opponent coming the other way. He is on schedule to flatten that puck carrier who is *caught in the trolley tracks*.

turnover *See also:* **giveaway**

turtle To avoid a fight by bending over and covering up, or even falling to the ice and exposing only a curled back to the aggressor.

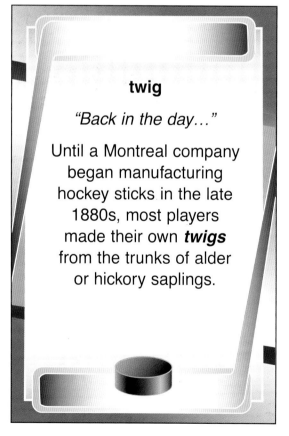

twig

"Back in the day..."

Until a Montreal company began manufacturing hockey sticks in the late 1880s, most players made their own *twigs* from the trunks of alder or hickory saplings.

twig A hockey stick. Derived from the traditional source of hockey sticks—trees. Of course, now many of the sticks used at higher, competitive levels are no longer made out of wood.

U

umbrella A power-play formation. The attacking team sets up inside the blue line with the players spread out in the shape of an umbrella: one on each *point*, two along the opposite *half boards*, and a man in front of the net.

undressed Made to look particularly foolish or inept because of the superior skill of an opponent. Usually describes an player who has been beaten very badly by the puck carrier in open ice, as a result of a nice *dangle*.

upstairs (1) High up in the press box area where the video-replay judges work. If there is some question as to whether or not the puck has gone in the net, the referee will *go upstairs* for confirmation or a second opinion.

(2) The upper part of the net. *See also:* **top shelf** and **roof**

V

"Sizing Things Up"

A regulation NHL puck
is 7.6 cm (3 inches) in
diameter, 2.54 cm
(1 inch) thick, and
154–168 g (5.5–6 ounces)
in weight.

vulcanized rubber (on a
string) The puck is made of
vulcanized rubber. If the vulcanized rubber is on a string, then
somebody is ***dangling***, or stick-
handling very cleverly to hang
onto the puck.

walk the line Move the puck parallel to the blue line. Often one of the point men will skate laterally just inside the offensive zone, looking for a shooting lane or an open man to dish the puck off to. *Skillins sends the puck back to O'Flurry at the point...he **walks the line**, he shoots...he scores!*

wall The area along the boards where there is Plexiglas, though it can refer to the boards in general.

wallpapered Flattened into the boards by a very hard body check, so that the player almost becomes a permanent part of the décor.

waltz in Skate in unopposed towards the net, carrying the puck.

waterskiing Skating up behind your opponent and hooking onto him with your stick so that you are being towed along. Definitely not allowed.
See also: **tailgating**

wheels going Skating really hard and fast. *Bonhom really has his wheels going tonight!*

wholesale changes A complete change of the three forwards and two defense, all at the same time.

wires it Shoots the puck very hard into the net.

wraparound A scoring attempt from behind the corner of the net. The puck carrier attempts to score by quickly swinging the puck around the net and just inside the post.

wrister A wristshot.

X

x-factor guy A very skilled or even dominant player who can win a game for his team with a tremendous individual effort. More commonly called an *impact player* or an *elite player*.

x on his back Refers to a player who has become a target for the other team to hit or otherwise gang up on, usually as a result of some unpleasant action on that player's part earlier in the game.

Y

yawning cage A wide open net for the shooter.

Z

Zamboni The special truck equipped to resurface the ice between periods.

JOHN GOLDNER grew up in the Town of Mount Royal, Quebec, where he was a regular on the outdoor rinks and at the recreation centre. John began playing minor hockey at an early age and continued competing in the TMR leagues until he was eighteen. As a youngster, John always rooted for the Montreal Canadiens, and his favourite player was Henri (Pocket Rocket) Richard. John currently resides in Montreal.

TED HEELEY is best known as an animation artist and sculptor. He has contributed his artistic talents to such television shows as *Sesame Street*, *Lunar Jim*, *Life's a Zoo*, and many more. His new animated television series, *Nerdland*, will air in Fall 2009. *Hockey Talk* is his first children's book. Ted lives in Toronto with his wife, Alex Moorshead.

For more *Hockey Talk* information and activities, visit

www.fitzhenry.ca/hockeytalk.aspx